FOR LEAH, WHO WAITED; M.I.B
FOR SOFIA, JOAKIM AND LAUREN; H.D.

HarperCollinsPublishers

No plain pets!

WORDS by MARC IAN BARASCH   pictures by Henrik DRESCHER

It's Time for a Pet,
I told Mom Last Night.
She Raised up One Eyebrow,
Then Said, "Well, ALL Right."

Flying Fish don't JUST
BLOW BUBBLES and STARE
THEY FLAP ALL THEIR Fins
And SOAR OFF Through The air!

WHEN the MOON'S A WHITE LAMP
AND THE SKY'S BRIGHT AND STARRY,
ME and MY CAMEL
WOULD go on SAFARI.

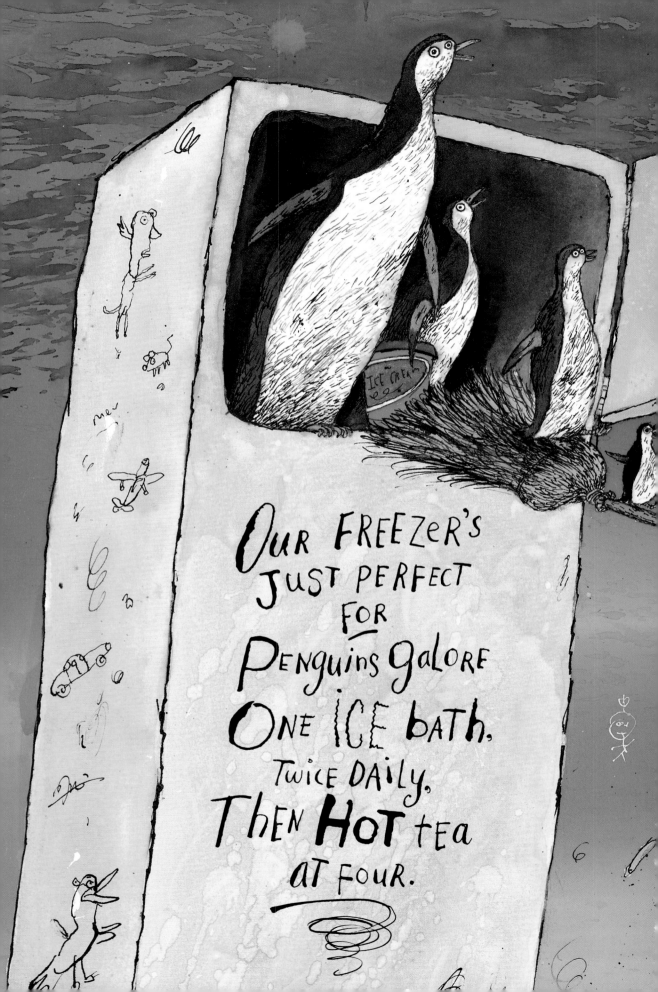

A JUNGLE SNAKE HUGS you
FROM EVERY DIRECTION
It's JUST A SNAKE'S WAY
OF SHOWING AFFECTION.

And DON'T BE SURPRISED IF I SAY HIPPOPOTAMUS.

A GOAT WOULD CLEAN UP
AFTER ME EVERY DAY:
LEGO BLOCKS,
DIRTY SOCKS,
GREEN CLUMPS
OF
CLAY.

A BAT'S a good bet. They're so CREEPY and SCARY! I'd have to put signs up TO WARN the TOOTH FAIRY.

And Burble and gurgle
And Jump Through a Ring.

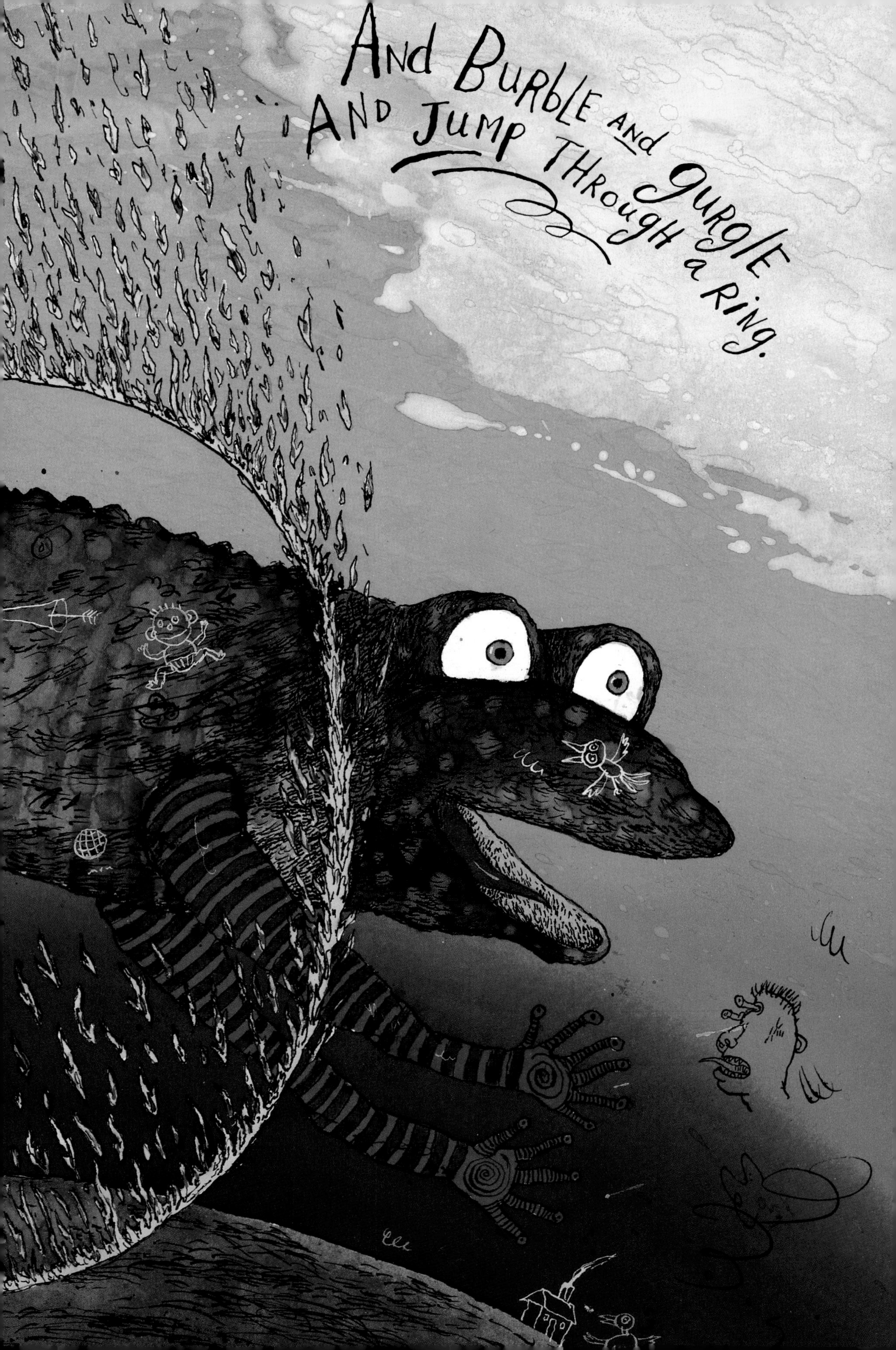

OR, WHAT ABOUT...
A THING THAT SINGS LULLABIES
UNDER THE BED
AND MOVES WITH SIX LEGS
STICKING OUT OF ITS HEAD,
THAT GOBBLES COLD CEREAL
RHUBARB AND RUBBER,
WHOSE ONE PART IS SKINNY
AND THE OTHER PART BLUBBER?
BUT MOM, THE MAIN THING
ISN'T REALLY WHAT KIND...

The main thing's I'll love him,

AS LONG AS HE'S
MINE!

Library of Congress Cataloging-in-Publication Data
Barasch, Marc.
    No plain pets! / words by Marc Ian Barasch ; pictures by Henrik Drescher.
       p.   cm.
    Summary: A child enumerates the many exotic pets there are from which to choose,
from big black gorilla to an imaginary thing with six legs sticking out of its head.
       ISBN 0-06-022472-X. — ISBN 0-06-022473-8 (lib. bdg.)
       ISBN 0-06-443375-7 (pbk.)
       [1. Pets — Fiction 2. Animals — Fiction 3. Stories in rhyme.]
    I. Drescher, Henrik, ill. II. Title.
    PZ8.3.B23434No 1991   90-22518
    [E]—dc20   CIP
                                                                  AC